Designed by Christy Warwick

Printed and bound in Hong Kong

Ask Fanny why, and
she'd gladly explain
That clothes, fancy clothes,
never did make the crane.

"You're too kind," said Fanny,
"but thank you my dears.
It cost next to nothing.
I've had it for years!"

She started a craze
among cranes everywhere
The natural look became
THE thing to wear.

Said Winifred whining,
    "It's highly unfair ~
You've outdone us all.
    Have an oyster eclair?"

    "Well really," trilled Carmen,
        "You've stolen the scene.
Where did you get it? Here,
        have some whooped cream."

Uccello said, "Whoop, girls,
here comes you know who...
Your outfit— why Fanny,
It's you, simply you!"

"Yes, charming," chirped Clarissa
"Tea? One lump or two?"

Then she powdered her beak and
flew straight out the door
Dressed in her feathers and
not a stitch more.

"Oh, but I would Mother,
for don't you see
Cranes were meant to be
fancy free!"

"Why nothing at all. I plan to go BARE."

"Shocking...a scandal... you just wouldn't dare! No one who's anyone goes anywhere bare!"

Fanny woke with a whoop,
feeling chipper and hearty.
"I must hurry," she said
"or be late for the party!"

"But Fanny," asked Mother,
"what will you wear?"

"Fanny, you're beautiful
just as you are.
You don't need new outfits
to make you a star."

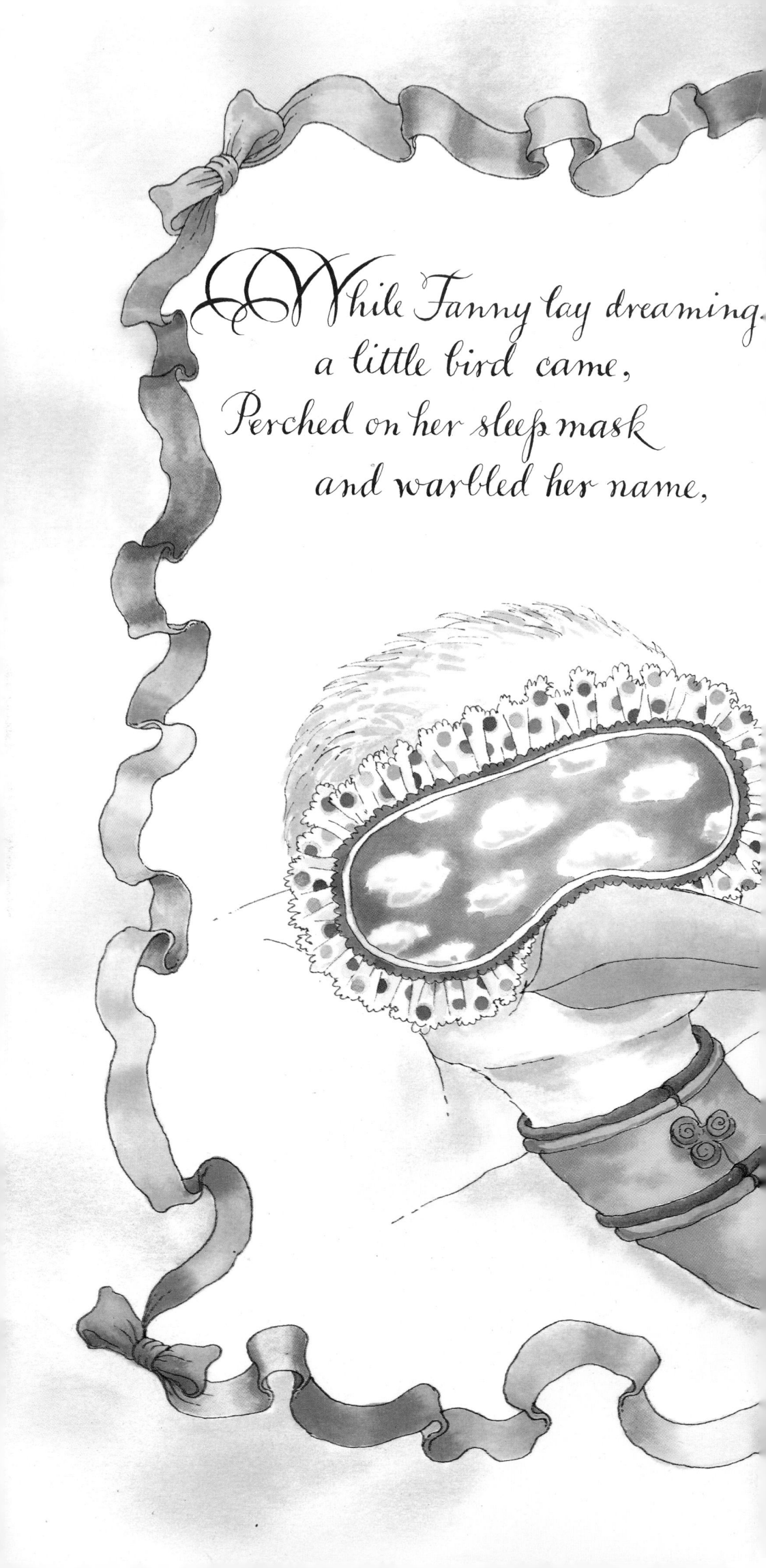

While Fanny lay dreaming,
a little bird came,
Perched on her sleep mask
and warbled her name,

"And now I regret I must
up and away,
For there's an emergency
I'd call to pay.

I must find that fellow,
Uncle McGrath,
He fractured his toe stepping
out of the bath."

Then tapping her knee with
a red rubber hammer;
He gravely announced in
his best birdside manner:
"She has a condition both
rampant and rare.
A well-advanced case of
Nothing-to-Wear."

Dr. Bill shut his satchel
and buttoned his vest,
Prescribed birdseed bouillon
and plenty of rest.

Dr. Bull scrubbed his wingtips
with medicinal soap,
saying, "There, there, no need
to abandon all hope."

And fearing her daughter
was frightfully ill,
She ran to the window
and called, "Dr. Bill!"

But, Fanny whooped weakly and fainted away.

"Your tufted tulle tutu, so sprightly, so gay...."

"These herringbone knickers
are naughty but nice."
"What! And be seen in
the same outfit twice!"

"Your thick satin jumpsuit
of pelican pink...?
Is in terrible taste.
What will everyone think?"

"Nothing to wear? Why that's
quite absurd.
You're known far and wide as
the town's best-dressed bird.
This peacock-blue ball gown
by Yves St. Je Rel
Looks rather fetching with your
French birdcage
hat."

"I'd sooner mud wrestle
before I'd wear that.
It pinches and scratches.
It makes me look fat!"

"This parrot-green tea gown
is delightful, divine!"
"It's horrid. It's florid.
It's last week's fashine!"

"Whoop, whoop and alas!
I'm in utter despair.
I waited to and fro and
I've nothing to wear!"

The most fashionable finds
about town will be there:
Winifred, Carmen, Noëlle
and Claire.

"Mother, oh Mother, come quickly!"
she cried.
Her mother at once flew to
her side.

She found Fanny feet up,
whooping with woe;
Swinging from the chandelier
by one dainty toe.

And there on the floor
in an opulent pile
Were outfits of every
description and style:

"Today, whoof! Good Heavens,
that's much, much too soon.
I'll never be ready by this
afternoon!

To:
My Fanny McFanny
Weeping Cane Square

Please come for tea and
oyster eclairs.
Wear your best frock & bring
your own chair! This afternoon
At a quarter to three.

Contessa Winifred von Carp
RSVP

While opening the
mail with her manicured
teeth,

A shocking pink
letter caused her to...

Each day she was swamped
with engraved invitations
To galas, regattas and masked
invitations.

At every affair she was
Lord of the ball,
Adored and admired
by one and by all.

Nightly

Morning,....

Fanny McfancY of
Keeping Crane Square
Was a rare bird of fashion,
a bird of great flair.
A chic bird who always
knew just what to wear.

Fanny did not wear her
fancy things lightly,
She changed outfits

Fanny McFancy

A Passion for Fashion

Text copyright 1988 by Patricia Thackray
Illustrations copyright 1988 by Sandra Forrest
The Grccn Tiger Press, Inc.
San Diego, California
First Edition
1　3　5　7　9　10　8　6　4　2

Library of Congress Catalog Card Number: 88-80420
ISBN: 0-88138-113-6

Special thanks to Fanny's first fan, Tim Gray.

Fanny McFancy for Fashion

The Green Tiger Press
San Diego
1988

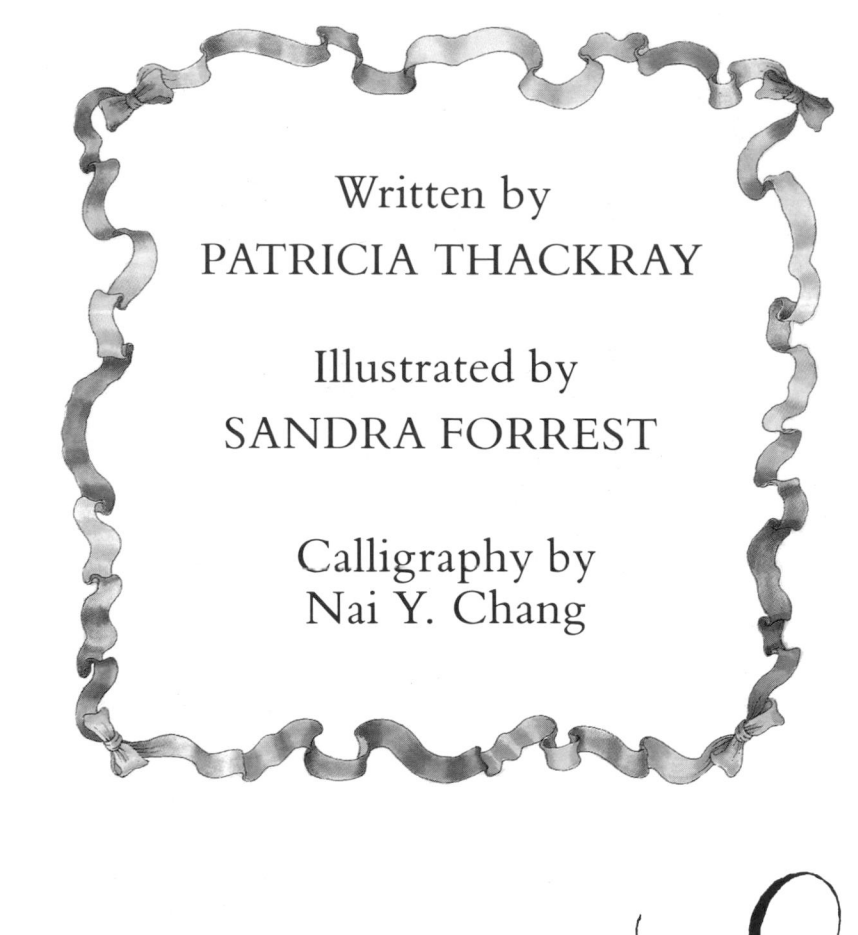

Written by
PATRICIA THACKRAY

Illustrated by
SANDRA FORREST

Calligraphy by
Nai Y. Chang

A passion

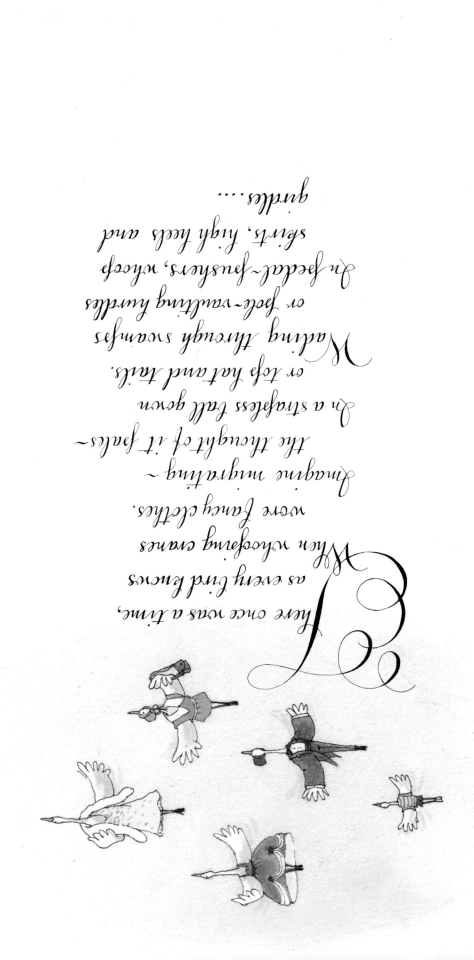

There once was a time,
as every bird knows,
When whooping cranes
wore fancy clothes.

Imagine migrating ~
the thought of it galls ~
In a strapless fall gown
or top hat and tails.

Wading through swamps
or foot-racing hurdles
In spiked-heel-sneakers, whoops
skirts, high heels and
girdles....